Bella Goes to School

Written By Ron Vietti

This book is based on the continuation of *Oreo Finds a Friend*.
To discover and purchase Bella's first adventure, go to
www.RonVietti.com.

Author Ron Vietti is the pastor of Valley Bible Fellowship, a church of about 10,000 people in Bakersfield, California. He is married to his lovely wife, Debbie, for over 40 years. Ron and Debbie have two children and four grandchildren.

Ron is the author of *Tribal Influence*, *Polyester People*, *Conspiracy of Silence*, and *Oreo Finds a Friend*.

You may contact Ron at www.facebook.com/PastorRonVietti.

For over 4 years, illustrator Tom Hollenbeck has been a youth pastor at Valley Bible Fellowship in Bakersfield, California. He is married to Justann for 2 years.

Acknowledgments:
I would like to give a special thanks to Tom Hollenbeck for the wonderful graphics and to Nicole Dickey for helping me with all the details of the book and study questions at the end. Great job, guys!
-Ron Vietti

Bella lives on the Simple Life Ranch with Rancher Steve.
They enjoy the ranch life.

They do ranch chores like taking care of the animals every day.

One day, Rancher Steve told Bella, "I think it is time for you to go to animal school while I go to work each day."

Bella had never been to school before.
This was a big moment in Bella's life!

When the first day of school came, Bella met several other students.
Oinky Pig and Sammy Squirrel were there, along with
Ducky Duck, Happy Horse, and Chicky Chicken.

They all lived on other ranches nearby.

Miss Barnhouse was the teacher at the school.

On the first day, she asked all the students
to share something that made them very happy.

Oinky Pig went first. He was very proud of his "oink."
He oinked for everyone, which made them all laugh.

He continued to "oink, oink, oink."
He said everyone who visited the ranch loved to hear him oink.

Next to share was Happy Horse. Happy Horse said he was really happy when children got on his back and he gave them rides all around the ranch.

Seeing the children smile made him very, very happy.

Then Sammy Squirrel got up and talked about
how well he could climb trees.

He took everyone outside and said, "Watch this!"

All the animals watched in amazement as Sammy climbed the tree really fast and then jumped from limb to limb... almost as if he could fly!

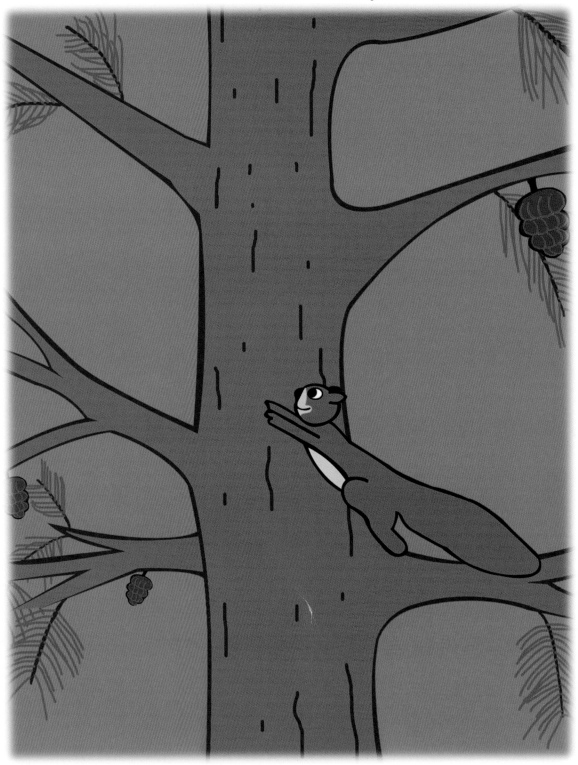

Sammy was really good at what he did.

Chicky Chicken then got up and showed
all the other animals how she could lay an egg.
It was a beautiful tan egg.

She told them how much everyone loved to gather her eggs.

Then it was Ducky Duck's turn. He took everyone to a pond and jumped in and swam in circles.

Back and forth he went, quacking all the while.

Then Ducky Duck did something that surprised everyone. He flew up high into the air. He flew round and round in circles. Up and down Ducky Duck went. Then he flew back down and landed in the pond.

There seemed to be no end to his talent.

Time ran out before Bella got her turn to share. Miss Barnhouse told Bella she would be the first one to share the next day.

The school day ended and everyone went home.

Bella went home and thought and thought about what her talent was.
The more she thought about it, the sadder she became.
"I have no talent," she said as tears began to form in her eyes.

Then the tears fell as she began to cry.

"I can't oink. I'm not strong enough for kids to ride on me. I can't climb trees like Sammy Squirrel. I can't lay eggs like Chicky Chicken. I certainly can't swim or fly like Ducky Duck. I am not good at anything.

I'm never going back to school.
Everyone is good at something except for me."

Rancher Steve came home from work and saw Bella's sad face.
"Why are you so sad, Bella?" Rancher Steve asked.
Bella replied, "I went to school and saw that all the other animals

are very good at many things, but I am not good at anything. I am
never going back to school again," Bella told Rancher Steve.

Rancher Steve felt very bad for Bella. Then he remembered about a book he had in the barn. It was called *Dog, Man's Best Friend*.

He brought the book and showed it to Bella.
Rancher Steve said "Bella, you have the greatest gift of all.

You have the gift of loving others and helping them feel good about themselves. Loving others, caring about them, and being a good friend are some of the most important things in life."

Then Bella was very happy. She always loved everyone, but she had never seen it as a gift that she was born with.

Bella didn't feel bad any longer about going back to school.

She would go back to school and love everyone there
and be happy for all of them.

So Bella went back to school the next day, taking the book with her.

She told the class that what made her happy was making others happy.

"Some people don't have friends," Bella said to the class,
"but I can be their friend."

And from that day forward Bella had five more friends.

They all loved Bella as much as she loved them.

The Real
SIMPLE Life Ranch

Happy Horse

Chicky Chicken

Author Ron Vietti
and Bella

Oinky Pig

Sammy Squirrel

Ducky Duck

Lessons from Bella

<u>Parents and Teachers</u>

Having two children, four grandchildren, and pastoring thousands of children, Ron Vietti desires to make sure each child understands how unique they are and the beauty they each have to offer the world.

The following curriculum was created to spark dialogue, both in the home and the classroom. You will find questions to ask, coloring pages that may be copied for use on regular paper, and exercises to help children understand the unique gifts that each one has.

Questions to Spark Dialogue

1. There are many reasons for going to school. Why do you go to school?

2. Everyone was born to be different. In what ways are you different from your friends?

3. One of the greatest things in the world is to love others and be their friend. Who are some of your good friends?

4. Which one of the animals do you like the most? Oinky Pig, Sammy Squirrel, Ducky Duck, Happy Horse, or Chicky Chicken? Why do you like that animal?

5. Rancher Steve helped Bella feel better when she was sad. Who helps you feel better when you are sad?

6. What is one amazing thing that you like about yourself?

7. How do your friends and other people help you feel happy?

Exercises for the Home or Classroom

Encouraging Words

Take a 4x6 picture of each child and glue it to the center of a poster board. Make one poster per child. Whether in a group setting or individually, allow each child to write positive words on each other's board that make the child in the picture unique. When completed, return each poster board to the appropriate child.

Exploring in Nature

Go outside and find animals, insects, birds, and other things that surround you every day. Discuss what makes each of them special.

Identifying Our Differences

Ask each child to write on a piece of paper what they like about themselves. Remember to provide enough time for the children to develop a thoughtful answer. Fold the paper and place it in a jar. Pull one of the pieces of paper out of the jar and ask if the children can identify who wrote it. Continue until all the papers have been pulled from the jar. Allow time for the students to discuss the differences they see in each other and how those differences benefit others around them.

Choosing to be a Friend

Bella made new friends with others who were very different from herself. Ask the children to find someone in the classroom whom they would like to know more about. Have them ask the student questions about what they like to do and what makes them happy. Allow enough time for them to get to know the other student better. At the beginning of the exercise, the teacher may have to show the students how to do this.

Drawing Exercise

Using your imagination, describe an animal that you would like to be. Draw a picture of your animal below. Describe all the things that make it unique.

Coloring Activities

Happy Horse

Chicky Chicken

Oinky Pig

Sammy Squirrel

Ducky Duck